Concert Night

Robert wanted to be a pilot.
He dreamed of flying low
over his little home town
when he was grown up.
Everyone would look up
and say,
"That's Robert Johnson,
you know.
He used to live here."

He read about planes
and dreamed about planes.
A pilot was the only thing
he wanted to be.

PILOT
HOW TO FLY
SUPER JETS
THE RED
PLANES

He did *not* want to be an actor.
But at this year's school concert,
the whole class was
to be in a play.
Robert had to say
only a few lines in the play
but he turned red
every time he said them.
He didn't want to stand up
in front of all the mothers
and fathers and aunts and uncles
on concert night.

CONCERT
NIGHT
R S T
U V W
X Y Z

Jane and Gloria teased him.
"Red hair! Red face!
Red hair! Red face!"

At every play practice,
he heard them giggling
as his face went hot.
He felt so silly
that he sometimes
forgot his lines.

"Robert Johnson,"
scolded the teacher,
"you have only a few lines.
Do wake up!"

Robert would try hard.
"It's a beautiful day, Sarah Sampson, don't you think?"

"Good, Robert, good," said Miss Holmes.
"Be ready for your next line."

Robert wished everyone in the school would get the measles.
No one even caught a cold.
He wished the hall would burn down.
But it didn't.
He dreamed of something really bad happening
—like a huge flood.
Life just went on.
The concert wouldn't be put off.

MEASLES! Everyone go home!

Concert night came.
The girls were wearing their best dresses.
The boys looked shiny from washing.
Everyone seemed happy and excited—
except Robert.
He sat in a seat,
feeling his
stomach churning.

CONCERT NIGHT
HALL

First, the choir sang.

After that, some children said a poem, while Robert's class got ready for their play.

And then — they were on!
Robert stood waiting for his turn.
His stomach seemed
to be doing somersaults now.

Suddenly Miss Holmes
was pushing him on.
"Now, Robert —
and don't forget your lines."

Robert tried not to look out
at the faces in the audience —
hundreds of faces,
all staring at him.
He kept saying his lines
over and over in his head.
He *knew* he would mix them up
when he said them out loud.

He tried his best.
"There's a . . . It's a beautiful day . . ."

He had forgotten!
He *had* to remember.
He *did* remember.
The words came in a rush.
"Sarah Sampson, don't you stink?"

A great gust of laughter swept the hall.
The children on the stage giggled.

Robert's face was so hot
that he thought it would catch fire.
Miss Holmes waved her arms and said,
"Carry on! Carry on!"

Everyone did.
Even Robert
said his other two lines,
but he remembered nothing
of the rest of the play.

Jane and Gloria
exploded with laughter
as he came off the stage.

Some of the other kids giggled
and said that terrible line to him.

Miss Holmes growled
when she heard them.
“It didn’t matter, Robert,”
she said to him.
“No one will even remember
that you made a mistake.”

Robert knew she was wrong.
They *would* remember.
Even when he was a pilot,
they would remember.
"That's Robert Johnson," they'd say,
when he flew over the town.
"He was in the school concert once,
and you'll never guess what he said!"

Robert never read another book
about planes or flying.
He started to read about
the Amazon.
When he grew up
he was going to go there
and look for lost tribes.

AMAZON
THE CONGO
AMAZON ADVENTURE
DISCOV
BRAZ

Robert thought that, if he was lucky,
he might get lost himself.
But even if he didn't,
one thing was sure.
In the Amazon jungle,
no one would ask him
to be in a play.